W9-CNC-517

The Collie of Castle Hill

The Collie of Castle Hill

Written and Illustrated
by
Christine Reilly Carter

Polt Mountain Press
www.poltmountainpress.com
P.O. Box 241, Califon, New Jersey 07830

text copyright ©2002 by Christine Reilly Carter
illustrations copyright ©2002 by Christine Reilly Carter

All rights reserved. No part of this book may be reproduced in any form
or by any electronic or mechanical means including information storage and retrieval systems
without permission in writing from the publisher,
except by a reviewer who may quote brief passages in a review.

Library of Congress Control Number: 2002105606

First Edition

Carter, Christine Reilly, 1951-
The Collie of Castle Hill
ISBN 0-9717964-0-8 Hardcover
ISBN 0-9717964-1-6 Paperback

Published by Polt Mountain Press
P.O. Box 241, Califon, New Jersey 07830
www.poltmountainpress.com
Printed in Hong Kong

For Carl in memory of Lucky
and for Alexis, Nicole, Michael & Tom
C.R.C.

One wintry night, as Carl and his father spread extra straw bedding for the cows, his father asked, "What would you like Santa to bring you for Christmas, son?"

"I don't think Santa can bring me what I really want," Carl replied.

"What might that be?" his father asked.

"I want a collie, Dad, just like the one on television. I want one of that collie's pups. I'd name him Lucky."

Carl's father stopped spreading straw and leaned on his pitchfork. "That's a mighty tall order, even for Santa. Would any other collie pup make you happy?"

Carl shook his head.

"I didn't think so," said his father. "Run along now, son. Your chores are done."

Carl ran across the snow-covered lane and into the warmth of the farmhouse. He glanced at the kitchen clock and quickly pulled off his work boots. His mother smiled and traded him a mug of steaming hot chocolate and a piece of warm gingerbread for his coat and scarf.

"You're just in time for your show, Carl," she said.

Carl's favorite television show was just beginning. Every Sunday evening, after his chores were done, Carl watched the adventures of the young boy and his collie. Often, the boy ended up in danger of one kind or another. His collie always ran and brought help just in time to save him. Lucky would do that, too, if Carl were ever in danger.

Every night Carl dreamed about adventures with his own collie, Lucky. He dreamed that he and Lucky played hide-and-seek in the woods beyond the meadow and that they swam and fished together in the Neshanic River. He dreamed that no matter what happened, he would be there for Lucky and Lucky would be there for him.

Each morning Carl awoke to find himself alone in his room. His dog, Lucky, lived only in the world of his dreams.

Carl lived on a small, isolated farm in New Jersey. He spent most of his time alone, doing chores and dreaming of Lucky.

Carl anxiously counted down the days until Christmas. He and his father cut a fir tree from the lower field. The smell of his mother's freshly baked cookies, pies and holiday breads found its way from the kitchen into every room in the house. Carl knew Santa would try his best to bring him the pup he wanted.

Carl's older brother had his heart set on a new fishing pole. He even helped Carl with the barn chores hoping to score extra points with Santa. At night, while Carl dreamed of adventures with Lucky, his brother dreamed only of catching fish.

Usually the family ate early on Christmas Eve. After dinner they would invite their neighbors to join them for coffee and sweets. This year was different. Carl's father worked as a carpenter as well as a farmer. He was working on a roof, quite a distance from the farm, and would not be home until seven o'clock. The table was set and the dinner kept warm in the oven.

At last Carl saw headlights coming up the lane. A few minutes later the front door opened and Carl's father walked in holding a rumpled carriage blanket in his arms.

From out of the folds emerged the small head of a collie. Smiling from ear to ear, Carl's father placed the collie pup into Carl's outstretched arms.

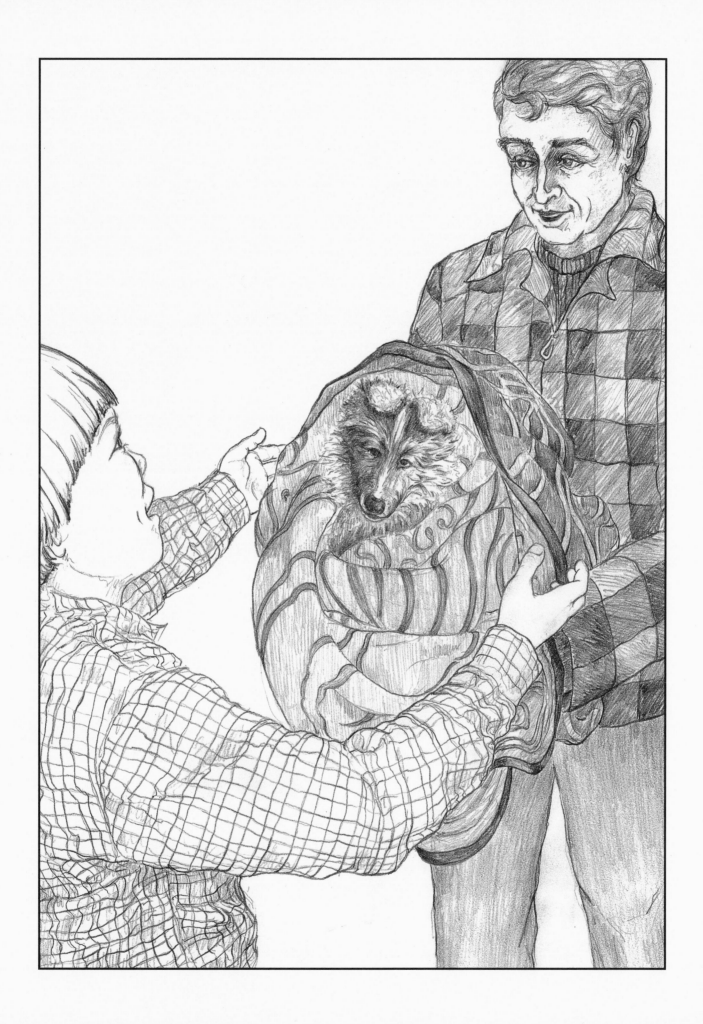

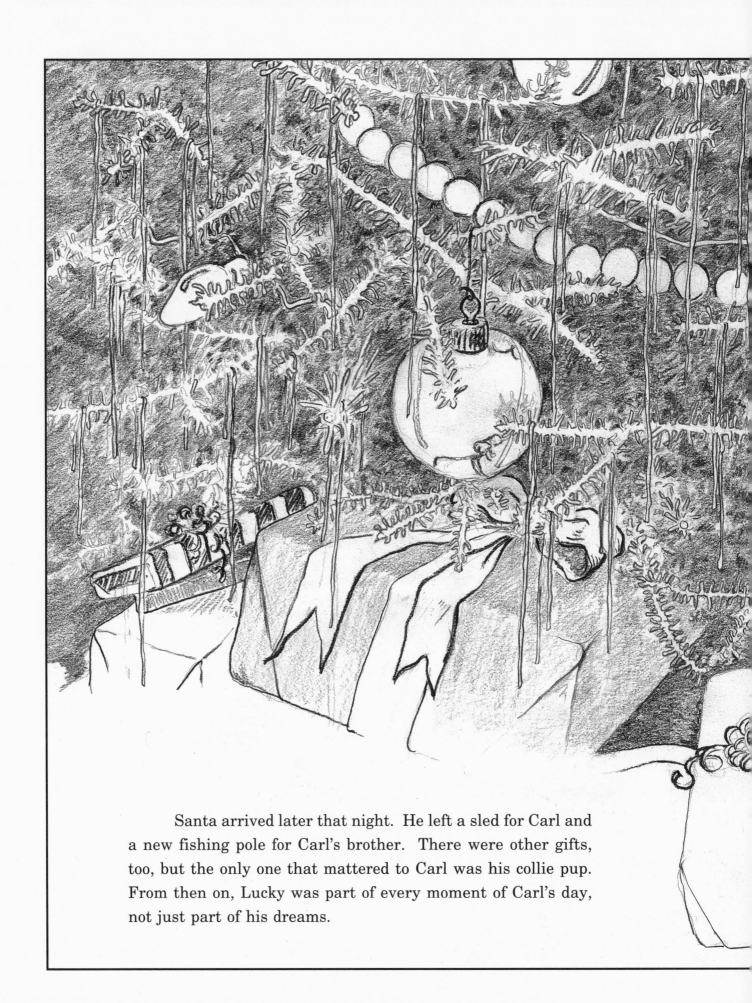

Santa arrived later that night. He left a sled for Carl and a new fishing pole for Carl's brother. There were other gifts, too, but the only one that mattered to Carl was his collie pup. From then on, Lucky was part of every moment of Carl's day, not just part of his dreams.

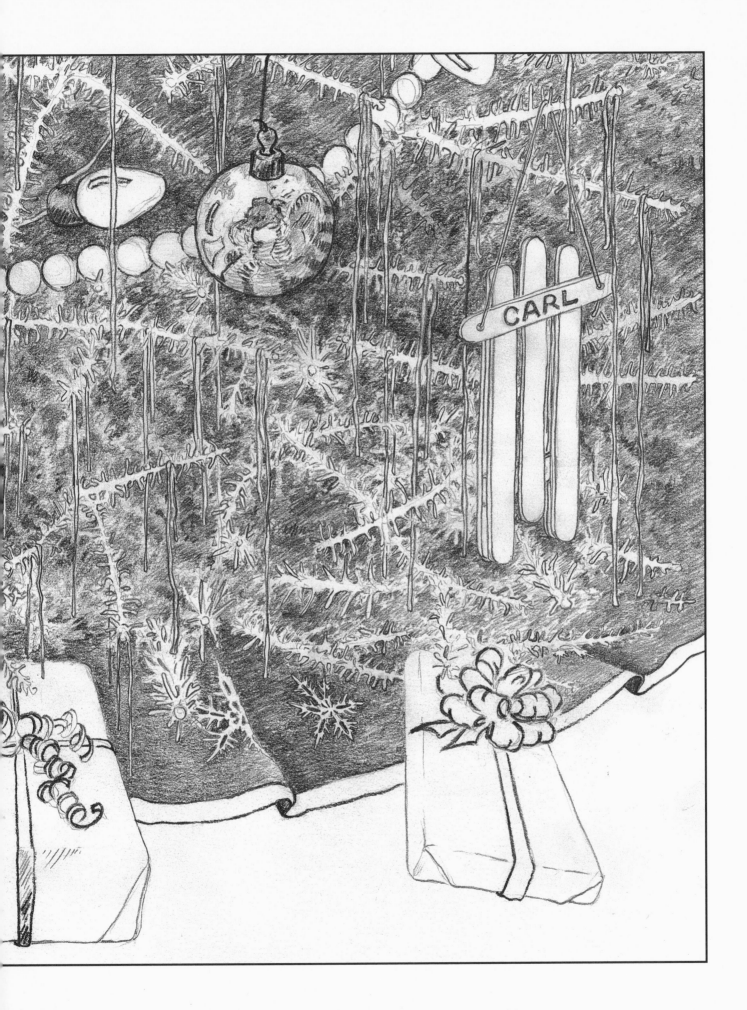

Winter passed. When Carl fed the cows and spread the straw, Lucky stayed by his side. When Carl stacked the firewood and shoveled the snow, Lucky followed him. When Carl slept at night, Lucky lay curled against his feet at the foot of the bed.

Spring rains and warmer weather covered the hills with a blanket of wildflowers. The two inseparable friends ran together through the high grass of the meadow. They played hide-and-seek among the trees in the woods behind the orchard. They chased harmless snakes out of the blackberry bushes and fished along the banks of the river.

Summer brought new games and adventures. Lucky had grown tall, his hair long and majestic. Hour after hour the two friends chased each other through the woods, across the fields, and over the meadow.

September arrived and Carl returned to school. Lucky lay beneath the big maple and watched and listened for the school bus that would bring Carl home to him.

Every day Lucky sat waiting at the end of the lane when the bus pulled up. Neither the bus driver nor the children on the bus would forget the rainy day when Lucky sat waiting for Carl, a yellow slicker held firmly in his mouth.

When Halloween came, Carl's mother was happy to have Carl go trick-or-treating with Lucky as his companion. Lucky was almost a year old. His thick, silky hair hung down beneath his strong chest. A fancy collar and a special tail easily transformed Lucky into a lion. Carl wore a tiger costume made from black and orange flannel. The felt mask stuck to his face as he breathed in the cold autumn air.

Together the lion and tiger courageously approached the house of Miss Hilary, the most feared schoolteacher in town. Miss Hilary lived alone. She was tall and thin with long, long fingers. Rumor had it that she was a witch. One slow step at a time, Carl and Lucky made their way to the front door and rang the bell. The door opened.

Miss Hilary offered Carl a treat, her long fingers wrapped around a homemade popcorn ball. Then she looked at Lucky. Nervously, Carl thanked Miss Hilary for the treat and turned to leave.

"Wait here," she said. Carl didn't dare disobey.

Miss Hilary returned. This time, her fingers wrapped
around a giant hambone. She knelt down and offered it gently
to Lucky. Miss Hilary didn't look scary at all when she smiled.

Winter returned, cold and snowy. One windy afternoon Carl and Lucky dragged the sled up the big hill for one fast ride down the slick, icy slope. Carl sat in the back with Lucky in front.

Down the hill they flew. Lucky's hair whipped at Carl's face. Their speed carried them beyond the bottom of the hill, up the rise by the pond and launched them out onto the thin ice. The ice cracked. Both Carl and Lucky fell through the cracked ice and into the freezing water.

Quickly escaping the shallow water, they walked back through the meadow of deep snow, dragging the sled behind them. By the time they reached the back door of the farmhouse, icicles hung from Lucky's chest. Carl's quilted leggings stood stiff below the knees and the metal clasps on his galoshes were frozen tight.

Half an hour later Lucky lay on the small braided rug in front of the fireplace. Carl sat beside him, scratching Lucky's favorite spot behind his ears.

Another spring bloomed with new adventures, farther from the farm. Carl and Lucky often looked for treasures along the railroad tracks and in the town dump. Lucky patiently watched Carl arrange the treasures in his private place behind the barn.

Summer finally arrived again. Carl's older brother went to Boy Scout Camp for a week and left his favorite fishing pole behind.

One day, Carl and Lucky found themselves home alone. Carl's father was working down the road, building a new porch for a neighbor. His mother had walked into town to help at a bake sale. It was a lazy summer afternoon, perfect for fishing.

Carl climbed the stairs and lifted his father's waders from the hook. He tied them tightly around his small waist with a length of clothesline. Then he tromped into his brother's room, opened the closet door and grabbed his brother's favorite fishing pole.

Carl and Lucky crossed the cornfield where their neighbor, Jake, was plowing, then followed the hedgerow down to the meadow filled with tall grass and buttercups. At the edge of the meadow lay the Neshanic River.

Spooky-looking trees lined the riverbank on both sides. Instead of growing tall and straight, the tree branches stretched out over the water as if to guard the secrets whispered to them by the slow-moving, strong current.

The two companions walked along the bank to Carl's favorite tree. Carl often fished from the bend in the old branch that hung down close to the water. He climbed up the trunk and inched out onto the branch. He held his brother's fishing pole carefully, fearing it might slip from his hand and be carried away by the river's current.

Lucky watched from high on the bank. Carl made sure Lucky stayed clear of the edge. Had Lucky come closer, he might have slipped down the muddy bank into the water.

Carl positioned himself comfortably in the crook of the branch. He was about to cast his line when he heard an awful cracking sound.

"Help!!!!" Carl screamed as he fell, along with the branch, into the cold water below.

Carl clung tightly to the branch. It had broken, but remained attached to the rest of the tree trunk by a few strands of healthy wood. The water rose to his shoulders, filling the waders still tied tightly around his waist. The weight of the waders threatened to tear him from the branch and pull him down into the depths of the river.

Lucky barked wildly, approaching the edge of the bank as if to jump into the water after Carl.

"No, Lucky!" screamed Carl. "NO! ... Get help! ... Lucky, go get help!"

In the distance he could still hear Jake's tractor plowing the upper cornfield.

"Lucky! Go get help!" Carl screamed again.

Lucky turned away from the bank and disappeared.

The water felt cold and heavy. Carl thought of nothing but holding tightly onto the branch and listening for Lucky's return. Would Lucky be able to bring help? Would help come in time? Would Lucky be like the collie on television, and know what to do to save Carl?

Just as Carl began to lose his grip, he heard Lucky's bark. With each passing second the bark grew louder and gave Carl the will and strength to hang on a little longer.

Lucky arrived first with Jake running close behind. Jake slid down the muddy bank to the water's edge. Still too far away to reach Carl, Jake stripped off his belt and threw it out toward Carl.

Holding even tighter with his right arm, Carl let go of the branch with his left. On the third throw, Carl caught the end of the belt. Jake dug his feet deep into the muddy bank and pulled as hard as he could.

Lucky barked furiously as Jake hollered to Carl to hold on. Carl felt the riverbed beneath his feet, but he kept slipping in the mud, losing his footing.

Finally, a wet, frightened Carl lay exhausted upon the muddy bank. Jake struggled to help him up to where Lucky paced back and forth. After Carl caught his breath, he reassured Jake that he was all right and could make it home safely. Before returning to his tractor, Jake untied the wet knot of the clothesline that still anchored the waders to Carl's small body.

Carl and Lucky walked back to the farmhouse by way of the creek rather than the meadow. They walked slowly — very slowly. The sun sank closer to the horizon and an occasional lightning bug flashed through the trees.

Carl was in no hurry to return home. He had lost his brother's fishing pole. It was either at the bottom of the river or downstream. He remembered it being jerked out of his hand as the branch broke. He had watched in horror as it fell into the water and vanished. Carl knew that if Jake told anyone what had happened that day, Carl would no longer be allowed to go alone to the river with Lucky.

That night, Lucky lay beside Carl instead of curled at his feet. Carl felt the rhythm of Lucky's heart beating beneath his fingertips. He fell asleep knowing that his collie, Lucky, had been there for him when he needed him most. Lucky was the best dog in the world.

The following day, Carl and Lucky returned to the river to hunt for the lost fishing pole. They found it washed up along the muddy bank with hardly a scratch on it.

Jake never did tell anyone about pulling Carl out of the
river. Years passed. Carl and Lucky had many more adventures
together, playing baseball, flying model airplanes and exploring
the woods. Many times they went fishing and swimming together
in the Neshanic River, but never again did Carl wear his father's
waders, or fish from an overhanging branch, or borrow a fishing
pole from his brother.

Lucky lived a long and happy life. Carl still remembers
him as the amazing Collie of Castle Hill, a hero, a companion,
and a faithful friend.

The End

Carl Maier and Rusty, August 2001
Pastel portrait of Lucky at Castle Hill Farm by Jerilyn Weber
Photograph by Debbie C. Wenzel

Author's Note

The Collie of Castle Hill is based on the real-life adventures of Carl Maier and his collie, Lucky. I wrote the story as a chronicle of the events that took place in the mid-fifties, as told to me by Carl. Due to the fact that the only witness to the fishing incident has long since passed away, I present this story as a work of fiction.

Carl has always believed that the pup his father brought home that Christmas Eve in 1954 was indeed the one and only pup Carl wanted, the son of the famous collie he watched on television. Fact or fiction, no greater love could have existed between a boy and his dog. There is no doubt that the bond between Carl and Lucky greatly influenced Carl's direction in life. In 1986 he began volunteer therapy work with Grendle, a Shetland Sheepdog. Since 1992, his dogs have all been certified therapy dogs. Carl's devotion to his animals and his dedication to bringing dogs and people together for companionship, comfort, and assistance is an inspiration to all who share this common goal.

Lucky
Collie 1954 - 1971
The Collie of Castle Hill

Grendle (left)
Shetland Sheepdog 1984 - 1996
Certified Therapy Dog
Tanya (right)
Shetland Sheepdog 1985 - 1988
Certified Therapy Dog

Tasha
Shetland Sheepdog 1986 - 1998
Certified Therapy Dog
Poster Dog for the
Make-A-Wish Foundation
of New Jersey
from 1992 - 1996.

Jeniffer
Shetland Sheepdog 1988 - 2001
Certified Therapy Dog

Jasper (left)
Pomeranian 1987 - 1997
Trooper (center)
Shetland Sheepdog 1987 - 1994
Grendle (right)
Shetland Sheepdog 1984 - 1996
All three were Certified Therapy Dogs

Jessie
Black Pomeranian 1994 -
Certified Therapy Dog

Amanda
Collie 1996 -
Certified Therapy Dog

Rusty
Collie 1998 -
Certified Therapy Dog
Designated as the
New Jersey Red Cross Mascott
due to his efforts
to comfort family members
of the victims of the
Septemeber 11, 2001 attack on the
World Trade Center, NYC.

Dear Reader,

There are many breeds of dogs that qualify as excellent therapy and service dogs. Therapy work is also performed by cats, rabbits and other trained pets. For further information and a listing of organizations that provide assistance in the training and certification of you and your pet, please visit the "related links" page on our web site at:

www.poltmountainpress.com

Special thanks to:
Bryce, Lee, Kevin, Michael, Nicole and Rusty
for your patience and cooperation as models for the
illustrations in
The Collie of Castle Hill.

C.R.Carter

Polt Mountain Press, Post Office Box 241, Califon, New Jersey 07830